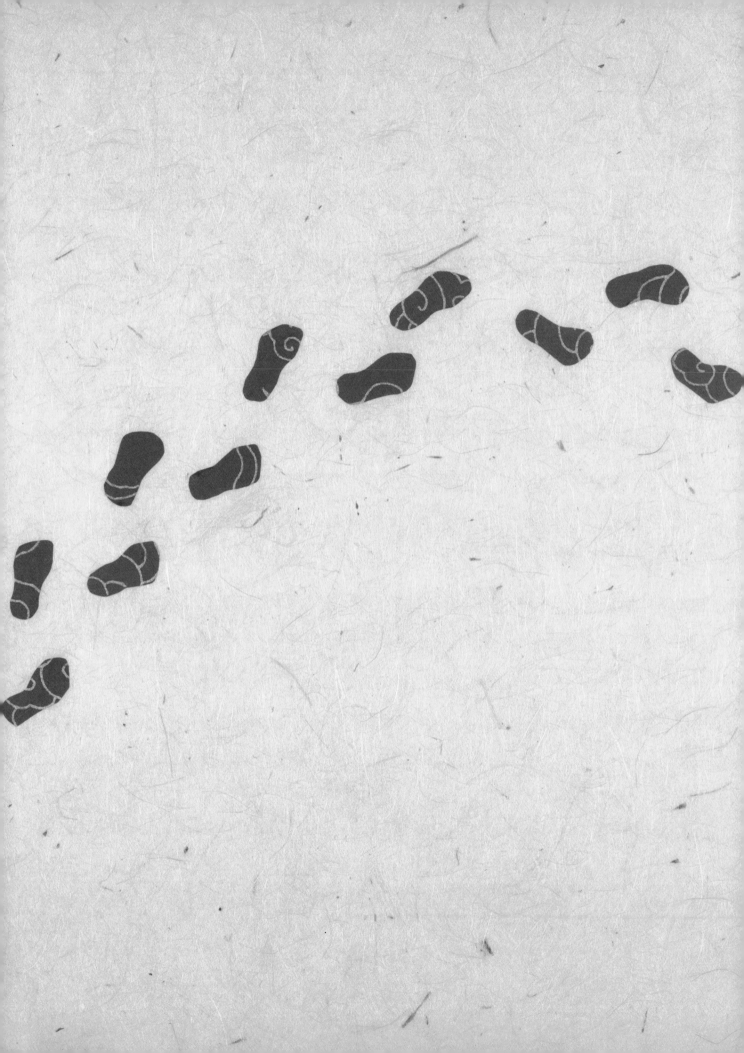

Steps and Stones

Steps and Stones

GAIL SILVER

ILLUSTRATED BY
CHRISTIANE KRÖMER

AN ANH'S ANGER STORY

**Plum
Blossom
Books**
Berkeley, California

The illustrations are collages combined with brush and pencil drawings

Text © 2011 by Gail Silver
Illustrations © 2011 by Christiane Krömer
Edited by Rachel Neumann
All rights reserved
Printed in China

Plum Blossom Books
P.O. Box 7355
Berkeley, California 94707
www.parallax.org

Plum Blossom Books is an imprint of
Parallax Press, the publishing division
of Unified Buddhist Church, Inc.

Cover and text design by Debbie Berne Design
www.debbiebernedesign.com

Library of Congress Cataloging-in-Publication Data

Silver, Gail.
  Steps and stones / Gail Silver ; illustrated by
  Christiane Kromer.
    p. cm.
  Summary: Angry at his friends for not wanting
to play his favorite activity, Anh is revisited by
Anger who demonstrates how mindful breathing
can soothe and transform strong emotions. Based
on teachings about mindfulness and Buddhism by
Thich Nhat Hanh.
  ISBN 978-1-935209-87-4 (alk. paper)
[1. Anger—Fiction. 2. Meditation—Fiction.
3. Vietnamese Americans—Fiction.] I. Kromer,
Christiane, ill. II. Title.
PZ7.S58567St 2011
[E]—dc22
                   2011000763

1 2 3 4 5 / 15 14 13 12 11

For Ben, and all of his earthly treasures —GS

To Leo and Diane Dillon, in everlasting gratefulness —CK

Recess
is Anh's favorite part
of the day.

But not today.

Today his friends Sam and Charlie ran right past him, not even looking his way.

"Wait!" Anh called. "We're supposed to dig. I brought shovels and everything."

"We don't want to dig," said Sam, bouncing a big red ball in the dirt.

"Yeah," echoed Charlie. "Digging is for babies. We're playing kickball instead."

Anh felt like he'd been punched in the stomach.
"I don't want to play kickball," he said. "I want to dig."

But Sam and Charlie were already kicking the ball around and Anh was left alone.

Anh walked to the shade of the oak tree, a salty tear rounding the corner of his lip. He leaned against the tree and watched as the tear made a tiny puddle in the dirt.

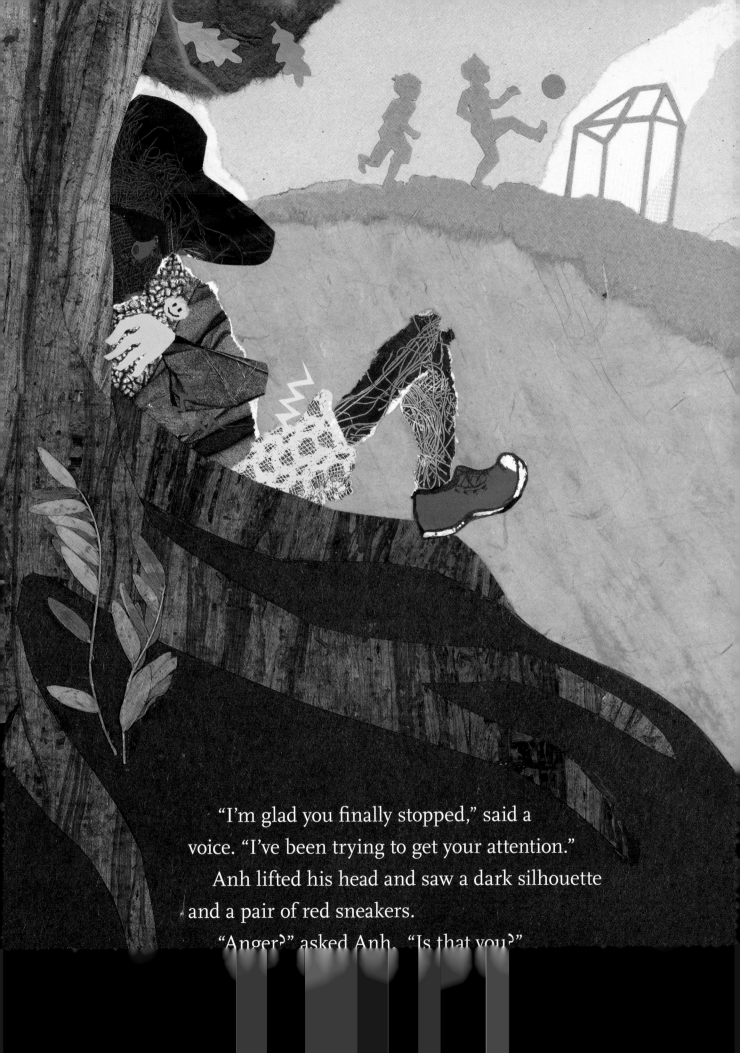

"I'm glad you finally stopped," said a
voice. "I've been trying to get your attention."
   Anh lifted his head and saw a dark silhouette
and a pair of red sneakers.
   "Anger?" asked Anh. "Is that you?"

"It's me!" said Anger. "You know I always show up when things aren't going your way."

Anh looked at his Anger. He hadn't seen him for a while.
"Why were you wearing all that stuff?" Anh asked. "I
almost didn't recognize you."

"I was trying to be inconspicuous," Anger whispered.
"I'm not sure if I'm allowed at school."

Anh and Anger sat together watching the other kids play kickball.

"Sam and Charlie were supposed to dig with me," said Anh.

"I know," said Anger.

"Now I have no one to play with," Anh said. "And Charlie thinks I'm a baby."

"I can think of a thing or two that I'd like to say to Charlie," said Anger.

"Me too!" said Anh. "I'd stand up to him and I'd say, 'I'm no baby!'"

"And then," said Anger excitedly, "we'd grab the ball and we'd throw it at him."

"Come on," said Anger. "Let's find Sam and Charlie."
Anger jumped up and started to run.
"I don't know," Anh said. "Maybe this isn't such a good
idea. Can we slow down?"

Anh and Anger began walking slowly together. With their first step, they took a breath in. With their next step, they let the breath out.

One step, breathing in.

One step, breathing out.

"I've never walked this slowly before," said Anger. "It feels funny."

"Let's try counting our steps," Anh suggested. "Maybe that will help."

One . . . Two . . . Three . . .

Anh and Anger quietly counted the rise and fall of each step.

Four . . . Five . . . Six . . .

Anh could feel his breath moving up and down in his belly.

Seven . . . Eight . . . Nine . . .

"It's hard to concentrate," said Anger. "I keep losing my count."

Ten . . . Eleven . . . Twelve . . .

Anh felt a cool breeze behind him, gently pushing him towards the field.

Thirteen . . . Fourteen . . . Fifteen . . .

The slow rhythm of Anh's breath comforted him and he started to feel better.

"Anger," called Anh. "Are you still here?"

"I'm right here," Anger answered softly.

"What are you doing?" asked Anh.

"I'm a little tired," said Anger. "I think I should stay here and rest."

"Okay," said Anh. "I can go on by myself now."

"Wait," said Anger, handing Anh a dandelion. "Make a wish."

Anh closed his eyes and drew in a big breath. He blew
it out and watched the dandelion seeds scatter.

"Now *you* make a wish," said Anh, turning to Anger,
but Anger had already faded away.

Anh rose to his feet and walked slowly towards the field. The sun was warm on his face and he wanted to play.

Sixteen . . . Seventeen . . .

Anh couldn't help walking a little faster.

Eighteen . . . Nineteen . . .

"Twenty!" Anh said, the sound of his voice surprising him.

"Twenty what?" someone asked. It was Sarah, a girl from his class.

"Um, twenty steps from there to here," said Anh. He pointed back towards the big oak tree.

"Why were you counting your steps?" she asked.

Anh thought about his Anger, the oak tree, and the slow walk. He thought about Charlie and Sam.

"It's a long story," he said.

"I like long stories," Sarah said, poking in the dirt. "Hey look what I found!"

"Wow!" said Anh. "That's a really cool rock."

Sarah held the small shimmery stone up to the sun and it sparkled in the light.

"I've never seen a rock like that before!" said Sam, running up.

"I know," said Anh. "You can find a lot of neat stuff when you dig."

"You haven't told us your story," Sarah said. "Why were you counting your steps?"

"Yeah," said Charlie, coming over. "Why were you walking so slowly?"

Charlie, Sam, and Sarah gathered around. "Come on," they said. "Tell us."

Anh looked at his friends and smiled.

"Recess is my favorite part of the day . . ." Anh began.

And it still was.

Plum Blossom Books

Plum Blossom Books publishes books for young people on mindfulness and Buddhism by Thich Nhat Hanh and other authors. For a complete list of titles for children, or a free copy of our catalog, please write us or visit our website.

www.parallax.org

Plum Blossom Books / Parallax Press
P.O. Box 7355
Berkeley, CA 94707

Tel: (510) 525-0101

Related Books from Parallax Press and Plum Blossom Books:

Anh's Anger by Gail Silver

Child's Mind by Christopher Willard

The Coconut Monk by Thich Nhat Hanh

Each Breath a Smile by Sister Susan

The Hermit and the Well by Thich Nhat Hanh

Mindful Movements by Thich Nhat Hanh

A Pebble for Your Pocket by Thich Nhat Hanh

Planting Seeds by Thich Nhat Hanh and the
  Plum Village Community

The Sun in My Belly by Sister Susan

Practice Opportunities with Children

Individuals, families, and young people are invited to practice the art of mindful living in the tradition of Thich Nhat Hanh at retreat communities in France and the United States. For information, please visit www.plumvillage.org or contact:

Plum Village
13 Martineau
33580 Dieulivol, France
www.plumvillage.org

Blue Cliff Monastery
3 Mindfulness Road
Pine Bush, NY 12566
www.bluecliffmonastery.org

Deer Park Monastery
2499 Melru Lane
Escondido, CA 92026
www.deerparkmonastery.org